AF598974

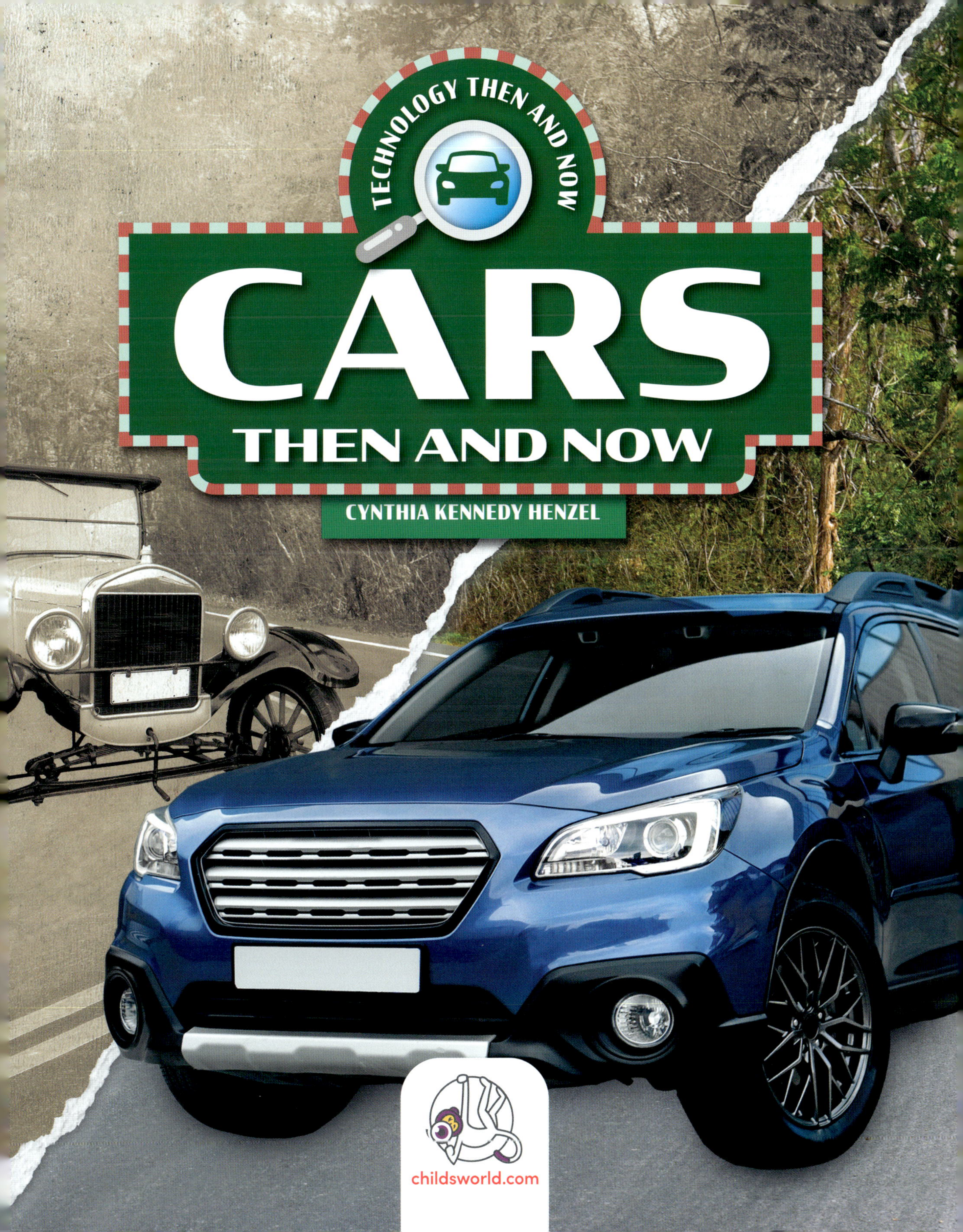
TECHNOLOGY THEN AND NOW
CARS
THEN AND NOW
CYNTHIA KENNEDY HENZEL
childsworld.com

Published by The Child's World®
800-599-READ • www.childsworld.com

Photography Credits
Photographs ©: Sanit Fuangnakhon/Shutterstock Images, cover (background), 1 (background), 3 (background); Margo Harrison/Shutterstock Images, cover (old car), 1 (old car); Shutterstock Images, cover (modern car), cover (icon), 1 (modern car), 1 (icon), 3 (icon), 4, 10, 16–17, 19, 20, 22; Kit Leong/Shutterstock Images, 4–5; Mercedes Benz/AP Images, 7; Everett Collection/Shutterstock Images, 8, 13; Sean Xu/Shutterstock Images, 15

ISBN Information
9781503889507 (Reinforced Library Binding)
9781503891128 (Portable Document Format)
9781503892361 (Online Multi-user eBook)
9781503893603 (Electronic Publication)

LCCN 2023950441

Printed in the United States of America

Cynthia Kennedy Henzel has a BS in social studies education and an MS in geography. She has worked as a teacher-educator in many countries. Currently, she writes fiction and nonfiction books and develops educational materials for social studies, history, science, and ELL students. She has written more than 100 books and 150 stories for young people.

TABLE OF CONTENTS

THE HISTORY OF

CARS

Cars have changed people's lives since they were invented in the late 1800s. Cars make it easy to visit friends and family. People drive cars to work. Cars take students to school and other activities. They make shopping easy. People drive cars on vacations. Cars have also had bad effects. They create air **pollution**. Accidents can cause harm. Today, people work to keep the good things about cars and fix the bad things.

Cars are a common sight in modern cities.

CARS CHANGE THE WORLD

In 1885, German inventor Carl Benz made the first modern car. At first, only rich people could afford cars. For short trips, most people still rode horses or used horse-drawn **carriages**. People rode trains for long trips.

Carl Benz (right) tested his car in October 1885.

BERTHA BENZ

Bertha Benz worked with her husband, Carl, to build cars. She decided to prove their new car worked. In 1888, she and her two sons made the first long-distance road trip. They traveled about 62 miles (100 km). It took 12 hours.

Families have been taking road trips for more than 100 years.

American inventor Henry Ford wanted to build a car that cost less. He invented the Ford Model T in 1908. It had no windows and no roof. But it was cheap.

In 1913, Ford had another idea to make cars cheaper. He started using assembly lines. On assembly lines, a car moved through the factory as each worker added a part to it. Now, Ford's factories could make a car in 1.5 hours instead of 12 hours.

Lower prices meant more families could afford cars. Farmers used cars to take crops to town to sell. People in rural areas drove to town to shop. People visited friends and family who lived far away.

By 1916, the United States had over two million cars.

Cars made busy city streets even busier.

Soon, cars packed the streets. They shared the roads with **trolley cars**, horses, bicycles, and people. Cars often had no safety equipment, such as brake lights. States had few traffic laws. Streets had no painted lines to mark lanes. Anyone could drive a car in most areas, even children. Bad drivers caused many accidents. Cars often killed children playing in the streets.

New York City and Detroit, Michigan, led the way to make streets safer. They passed laws that set speed limits. They required drivers to get a license. In the mid-1920s, the United States created traffic safety rules. Cars had to have safety equipment, such as headlights. These new laws made cars safer.

THE FAMILY CAR

Ford believed that the Model T was the only car that any family needed. But in the 1950s, people wanted nicer cars. Car companies began making bigger cars with bigger engines. New features were added, such as power steering. This made cars easier to drive. **Chrome** made cars fancier. These new cars used a lot of gas, but gas was cheap. People in the 1950s loved bigger cars.

People sit in their cars to watch movies at drive-in theaters.

DRIVE-IN MOVIES

Drive-in movies were popular in the 1950s. Drive-in movies had a big screen outdoors. People could drive their cars into a parking area. They parked next to a speaker. Then they could sit in their cars and watch a movie. It was cheap entertainment for families or people on dates.

Cars changed where people lived. Many people who could afford cars moved to **suburbs**. Suburbs had new homes, stores, and schools. A parent often drove to a job in the city. But the rest of the family spent their time in the suburbs.

Not every road in the United States was safe to drive on. Some roads were very narrow. Some bridges were very low. President Dwight D. Eisenhower wanted a new system of highways. He worried that military vehicles could not move quickly across the country in an emergency. In 1956, the United States began building the Interstate Highway System.

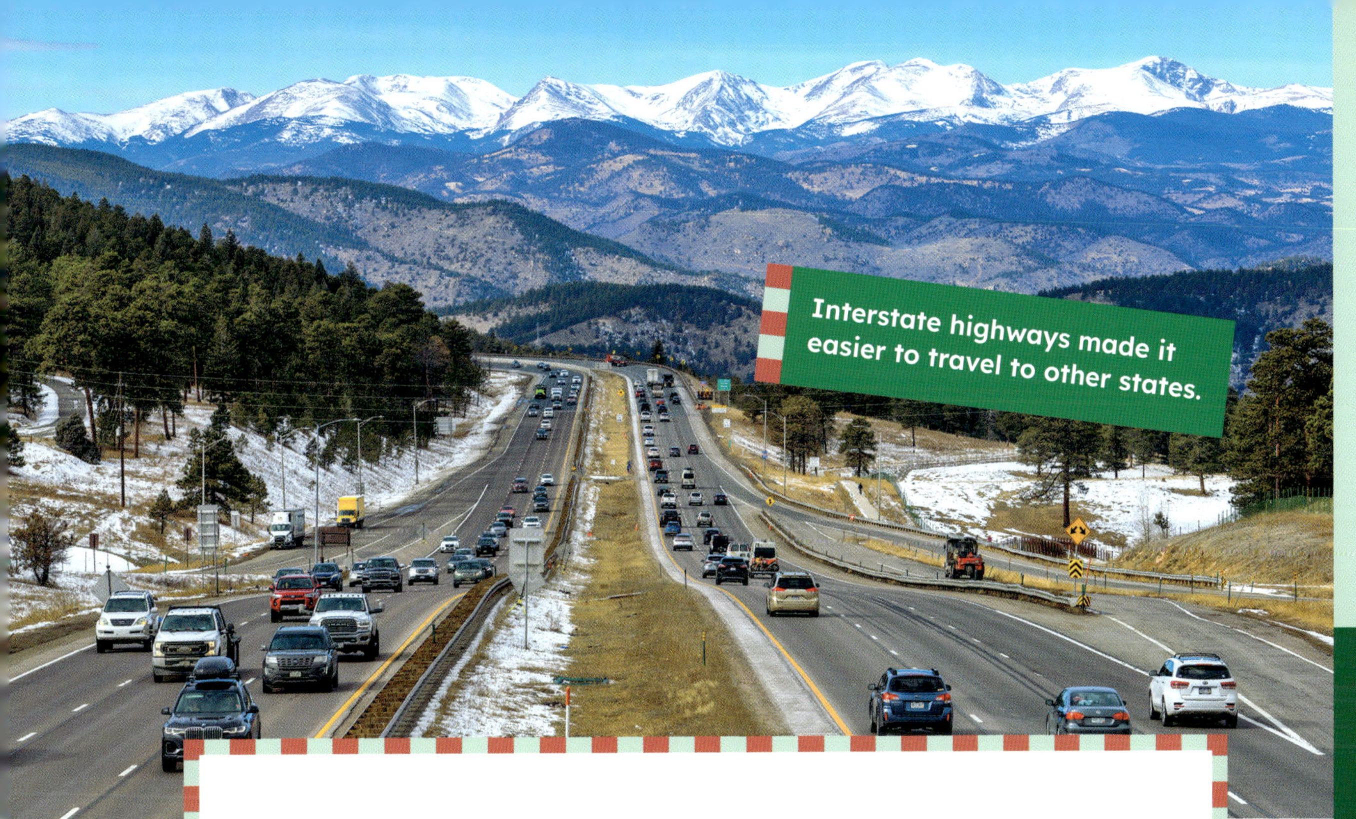

Interstate highways made it easier to travel to other states.

The new highways made traveling by car easier. New businesses opened along the highways to sell gas and car services. More hotels and restaurants for travelers opened.

The demand for big, powerful cars fell in 1956. Egypt blocked the Suez Canal, which carried much of the world's oil. Oil is used to make gas. Oil prices increased. People bought fewer cars. Companies began making smaller and more **efficient** cars.

CHAPTER 3

TODAY'S CARS

In 2021, more than 91 percent of all families in the United States owned cars. Thirty-one percent of families had two cars or more. People may have an SUV for family travel. They may have a smaller car for **commuting**. They may have a pickup truck to haul things. For most people, cars are an important part of life.

Cars have become safer. The US Congress created the Department of Transportation in 1966. One of its missions was to make cars safer.

Crash test dummies are used to test a car's safety.

Today, the National Highway Traffic Safety Administration tests cars to make sure they are safe before they can be sold.

Seat belts and other safety equipment were invented in the 1950s. However, not all people used seat belts. State laws now require people to use them as well as other safety equipment, including child seats. States passed laws against driving while **intoxicated**. In many states, it is illegal to text while driving. These laws have lowered the number of people killed by cars.

Seat belts help keep people riding in cars safe.

Cars still cause problems. Cars that burn gas release pollution into the air. Air pollution can cause illnesses, such as cancer. Air pollution also harms Earth by making it warmer. In response to these problems, companies have created more efficient engines. Still, the amount of pollution from cars is dangerously high.

GASOLINE CAR VS. ELECTRIC CAR

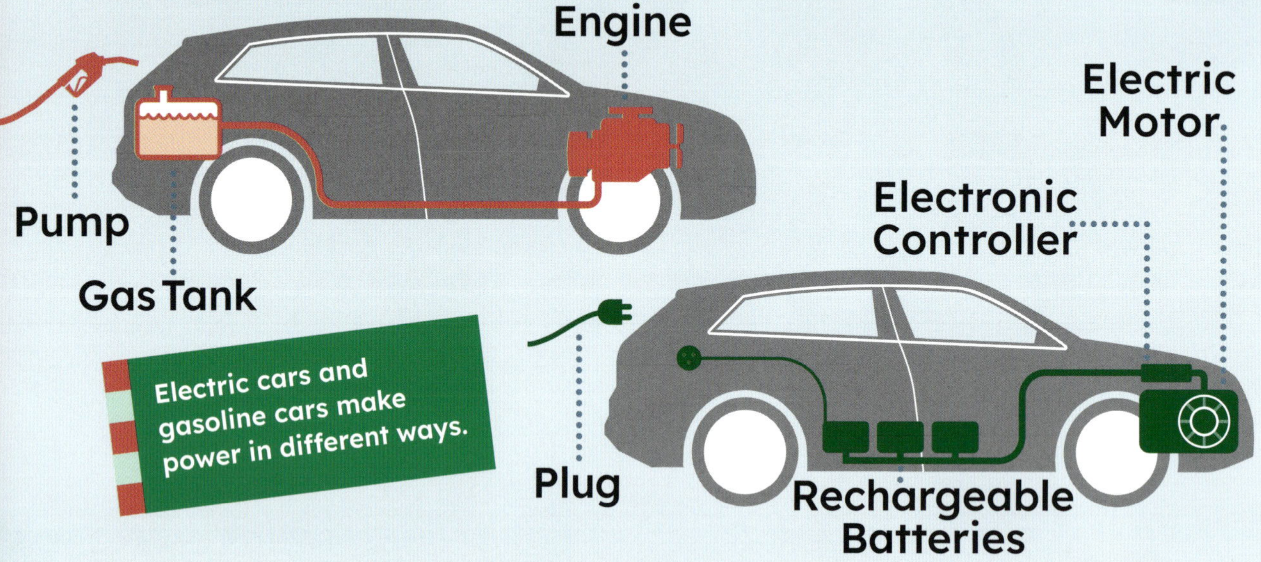

New cars often use other forms of power. Electric vehicles (EVs) use electricity. Hybrid cars use both electricity and gas. EVs and hybrids are less polluting than gas cars. One problem with EVs is that they need **recharging**. People need a place to plug in their cars at home and when traveling. In 2022, more than 12 percent of new vehicles sold in the United States were electric or hybrid. As places to recharge become more common, the number of EVs sold is expected to rise.

WONDER MORE

Wondering about New Information

How much did you know about the history of cars before reading this book? What new information did you learn? Write down three new facts that this book taught you. Was the new information surprising? Why or why not?

Wondering How It Matters

What is one positive way that cars affect your life? What is one negative way that cars affect your life? If you cannot think of a positive or negative effect, imagine how cars might affect other kids. What impact might cars have on their lives?

Wondering Why

Cars cause dangerous pollution. How do you think people can balance the convenience of cars with a clean environment? What is the impact of using cars less?

Ways to Keep Wondering

Governments have passed laws to solve many of the problems caused by cars. After reading this book, what questions do you have about cars today? What can you do to learn more about issues concerning cars?

FAST FACTS

- Cars were invented in the late 1800s.
- Henry Ford invented the Ford Model T, the first affordable car.
- Early cars and drivers caused many traffic accidents.
- Governments created traffic laws to make streets safer.
- In the 1950s, cars became bigger and easier to drive.
- People with cars often moved to suburbs.
- In 2021, more than 91 percent of US families owned cars.
- Cars create pollution that causes disease and harms Earth.
- Newer cars are safer and more efficient than older models.
- The number of people buying electric and hybrid cars is increasing.

GLOSSARY

carriages (KAYR-ij-iz) Carriages are four-wheeled vehicles usually pulled by two horses. People rode in carriages before there were cars.

chrome (KROHM) Chrome is a metal known for its shiny appearance. Some car bumpers are made of chrome.

commuting (kuh-MYOO-ting) Commuting is traveling a distance between home and work or school. Cars are commonly used for commuting.

efficient (eh-FISH-unt) Efficient means working in a way that gets a job done while using less energy. New car engines are more efficient than older engines.

intoxicated (en-TOK-sih-kay-tid) Intoxicated means to be under the influence of alcohol or drugs. Driving while intoxicated is a crime in the United States.

pollution (puh-LOO-shun) Pollution is something harmful added to the environment. Gas cars add pollution to the air.

recharging (ree-CHAR-jing) Recharging means to return power to a battery by using a different source of power. Electric vehicles need recharging.

suburbs (SUHB-urbs) Suburbs are areas where people live outside of a larger city. Roads connect a city to its suburbs.

trolley cars (TRAH-lee KARZ) Trolley cars are public transportation that run on electricity from overhead wires or tracks on the street. Trolley cars are an alternative to cars in some cities.

FIND OUT MORE

In the Library

Duling, Kaitlyn. *Cars*. Minneapolis, MN: Bellwether Media, 2022.

MacCarald, Clara. *Trains Then and Now*. Parker, CO: The Child's World, 2025.

Twiddy, Robin. *How Cars Changed the World*. Minneapolis, MN: Jump!, 2024.

On the Web

Visit our website for links about cars:
childsworld.com/links

Note to Parents, Caregivers, Teachers, and Librarians: We routinely verify our web links to make sure they are safe and active sites. So encourage your readers to check them out!

INDEX